Gofrette
Gets Wet

To our families

Editorial Directors
Jocelyne Morissette
Caroline Fortin

Translator
Gordon Martin

Graphic Design
Anne Tremblay

Page Layout
Lucie Mc Brearty

Retouching of images
Josée Gagnon

Copy Editor
Jane Broderick

Canadian Cataloguing in Publication Data
Michot, Fabienne, 1964-

    [Gofrette une leçon de plongeon. English]

    Gofrette Gets Wet.

    Translation of: Gofrette une leçon de plongeon.
For preschool children.

    1. Marineau, Michèle, 1955- . II. Brasset, Doris, 1958- . III. Title. IV.
Title: Gofrette une leçon de plongeon. English.
Français.
PS8576.1267G6313 1998   jC843'.54   C98-940372-6
PS9576.1267G6313 1998
PZ7.M52Go 1998

Canadä

We acknowledge the financial support of the
Government of Canada through the Book Publishing
Industry Development Program (BPIDP) for our
publishing activities.

Le Conseil des Arts | The Canada Council
du Canada | for the Arts

QAInternational gratefully acknowledges the
support of : The Canada Council for the Arts.

QA International
329, rue de la Commune Ouest, 3e étage,
Montréal (Québec) H2Y 2E1 Canada
T 514.499.3000 F 514.499.3010
www.qa-international.com

©1999 QA International

Printed and bound in Canada

10 9 8 7 6 5 4 3 2 1 02 01 00 99

Gofrette
Gets Wet

Doris Brasset and Fabienne Michot

QA INTERNATIONAL

Gofrette was born in a daisy. He had a big, big head and a little tiny body. He grew and grew and grew till his head sat on top of his body like a cherry on top of a chocolate sundae.

Blue and me in Paris

Long Ears

Red

Filo

Garbanzo

Blue

Gofrette had many friends: Red the Refrigerator, Blue the Dog, his bunny rabbit Long Ears, Filo the Lazybones and his cousin Garbanzo. Above all, he loved playing with Blue. Blue had such strong ears!

Red the Refrigerator lived in Gofrette's kitchen. They spent a lot of time together, discussing life's important questions.

Garbanzo El Magnifico, Gofrette's cousin, was in the circus. He was the strongest trapeze artist in the land of Zanimo.

One morning as Gofrette was having breakfast, Blue came to the
window with a letter in his paw.

"Good morning, Gofrette. I picked up your mail for you."
"Fanks, Brue. I'll wead it affa breakfiff," Gofrette replied, his mouth
full of pancake.

Gofrette got up and opened the window.
He shouted, "Blue, **BLUE, WHERE ARE YOU?**
My cousin Garbanzo wants me to join the circus
as a diving cat!"

"Wow! That's great, Gofrette," said Blue, hanging upside down from an apple tree. "I didn't know you could dive!"

"Well...I can't really...but...I thought you might show me."

"Of course I will. Let's go to the pool right away."

And off they went.

"Two tickets, please," said Blue to the Yellow Guy in the booth
at the pool.

Gofrette had run ahead to the turnstile. Obviously he had not read the **RULES AND REGULATIONS**.

"First things first. To the showers," said Blue.

Gofrette was getting a funny feeling in his stomach — and it wasn't his breakfast. Maybe this wasn't such a good idea after all.

Blue was ready to dive. "And now, just watch me carefully..."

Blue took a deep breath. He sprang off the diving board like a rocketship, with a **BOIoiOING** and a **BANG**,

twisting and twirling like a pretzel in the sky. **Oohs** and **aahs** were heard for miles around.

"Voilà!" exclaimed Blue. "Your turn now!"

Gofrette climbed onto the diving board.

"Take off your lifejacket, Gofrette! You know how to swim," said Blue.

With all of his courage and cat fat, Gofrette jumped off the diving board.
Arms, legs, paws and fur went flying!

Sky, sun, clouds, bugs and birds twirled around his head, and then there was a big **PLOP! SPLASH!**

Gofrette had just done the biggest bellyflop
Blue had ever seen.

"Oh, what a...special...performance...so...artistic,"
muttered Blue.

"I'll never be able to dive like you," whimpered
a sad Gofrette.

And then a little bird whispered a secret in his ear.

Up he got and tried again.
"AAAAAAH..."

Blue could barely look at his friend. Gofrette had
swallowed half the pool! He was so angry that he
screamed, **"I HATE DIVING, I HATE SWIMMING AND
I HATE WATER!"**

Fortunately, Blue knew exactly what to do to calm Gofrette down.

"Ah...much better," sighed Gofrette as he licked a delicious
strawberry ice cream cone.

Dear Garbanzo,

I had my very first diving lesson today. I got really wet. So did everyone else. I will be needing a few more lessons before I can join the circus. Blue says I am an artistic diver. I can't wait to show you. See you soon.

All my flops,
    Your cousin, Gofrette

Par avion

He might be fat but he floats.